WOODY AND JUNE VERSUS THE FUNGUS-HEAD ZOMBIES

WOODY AND JUNE VERSUS THE FUNGUS-HEAD ZOMBIES

WOODY AND JUNE VERSUS THE APOCALYPSE, EPISODE 2

ROBERT J. MCCARTER

LITTLE HUMMINGBIRD PUBLISHING

WOODY AND JUNE

VERSUS

THE APOCALYPSE

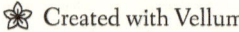

CHAPTER ONE

JUNE'S too much for me. She is. And I'm freaking out a bit.

"Look, Woody, just relax." She's behind me and touches my shoulders which are hard as cement and have been since the zombie apocalypse started.

I mean, yeah, she's cute, she's funny, she sometimes laughs at my lame jokes. And she's got those ocean blue eyes, that short black hair, that petite body and pixie vibe, but...

"Take a deep breath, bend your knees, don't lock your elbows, and slowly pull the trigger."

I lower the gun, a 9mm handgun of some sort, and look at June. Her face is hard, she's focused. We're in the high desert north of Flagstaff, Arizona, at an overlook to the Little Colorado River Gorge. It's fairly flat, great visibility, and the right kind of place to make noise in this new world. We've got some cans setup on a big tan sandstone boulder for me to shoot at.

We're fifty miles away from where we've been staying, and if the noise attracts Zs, we'll see them coming and be able to get away in time. And if the noise attracts humans... well, that can get trickier, but we won't be here much longer.

We're in the top of the parking lot of the overlook. A small tribal park on what was the Navajo Nation. Well, I don't know, still could be the Navajo Nation, but right now it's just June and me. Below us are old wooden stalls where the Navajo used to display their wares—turquoise and silver jewelry, pottery, and all kinds of touristy kitsch. Below that is the river gorge, deep, sheer, and dramatic, eroded by the Colorado's little sister through limestone and sandstone.

For the last few hours she's drilled me on the basics with an unloaded gun. It's now loaded and it's time for me to fire a gun for the second time in my life.

She's all of five foot two with her hands on her hips as she studies me and chews on her lower lip. We've known each other for four days now and in that time, she saved me from a zombie—by shooting it in the head and showering my face with zombie goo—and I saved her from a psychotic, petty, wannabe warlord with a manic, all-night prep session and an epic bluff against a bunch of armed men. But, I had, admittedly, gotten us into that mess.

There was a moment when our escape was assured that felt like... well, there was a peck on the cheek and laughter and hope. Hope for a future, a life worth living when most of the living are now the undead.

But this gun thing. She's good with guns, and by good, I mean "oh, my God, I didn't know people could really shoot like this, I thought it was just a Hollywood thing." She's good with a rifle at long distance, she's good with a pistol at close range, she's accurate, she reloads quickly, and she can take the gun apart blindfolded, clean it, all the while tap dancing to Queen's "We Will Rock You."

Okay, okay, I made that last part up.

"You have to be able to defend yourself," she says, still studying me. I get the impression that she is constantly reevaluating me. She trusts me—in so far as I don't mean her any harm and will put my life on the line for her—but other than that, I think her estimation of me has varied quite a bit.

"I don't like guns," I say.

And I guess my estimation of her has varied a bit too. It was like, "she's cute," to "my God she's cute!" to "wow, she just laughed at my joke, this is one post-apocalyptic babe... but, how long until she figures out how lame I am and moves on?"

"Why?" she asks. Lips are pursed and hip is cocked now. It's warm out here and gone is the grey oversized sweater she was wearing when we met at the dog food factory and she's got on jeans and a long-sleeve, navy-blue running shirt that hugs her petite torso. God, she's an athlete too. But after my long go-it-alone-no-matter-what phase, she's basically the most beautiful girl on planet earth to me. And she's a bit like Linda Hamilton's Sarah Connor in *Terminator* 2, although younger, and definitely cuter, and... well... it's attractive, *very* attractive, but it's rather intimidating.

"Guns kill people," I say with a shrug.

"Guns kill Zs," she counters.

"I know. It's just..." We haven't talked about our pre-apocalyptic lives. We've just avoided it. To me, those lives, those people, and that world is gone. We've all seen some bad shit, done some bad shit, and we've all lost too much. Some of it weighs on me, but talking about it doesn't seem like it's going to do any good. "I..."

"Come on, Woody, spit it out."

I bite my lip and shake my head, my eyes roaming from the gorge below us, across the gravel parking area, to the rough desert hills above us and Route 64 we came in on. While my mind is divided between cute June and "I hate guns," I'm still keeping an eye on things—I don't want to be surprised by the living, or the undead. "I would have to delve pretty deep into my past," I say, my eyes finding her round face, "pre-Z life, and..."

And I don't want to tell her what I did, not even this one, which is understandable. I mean, I was only six. My four-year-old brother and I were playing Cowboys and Indians and I knew that Dad kept the gun in a locked drawer of his desk. For once it was unlocked and I wanted something better than the pitiful plastic gun I had with the melted end—a candle experiment I had done a few months previously.

My brother had a toy bow and arrow, he hit me in the head with an arrow while I was holding the gun and I squeezed the trigger. It went off and went flying out of my hand. I didn't mean to...

June nods, her eyes finally looking away from me. She gets it. Dredging up the past can get in the way of surviving the present. Cute women, I might add, can get in the way of surviving, but are a lot more tempting than the past. A lot more.

"Besides," I add, "knives and bats work fine on the fungus-heads."

Her forehead crinkles and she's staring at me. "Fungus heads?"

I nod. "Yeah, the Zs, the dead. Their brains turn into this big ball of fungus, kind of like a head of cauliflower. Didn't you ever notice?"

She shakes her head.

I hold my hands out, palms up, and smile. "See... too much shooting, not enough bat swinging."

"You're serious?"

I nod. "Yeah. Not like the TV shows where it was some mysterious virus or something that didn't make a damn bit of sense. I think it's a parasite. There has to be something that digests what the Zs eat, give them energy to move their muscles, drives them to spread the infection. You've noticed that they move better once they've been dead a while, right? Seen that the ones that have bled out don't move so good?"

She blinks, her face blank. And then she's giving me that reappraising look again. I think I just went from "wimp who is afraid of guns" to "brainiac who has a theory on how the Zs work."

"Okay," she says with a sharp nod. "You're going to show me. Where can we find a Z around here?"

"Now?" I ask. I mean, we're in the middle of dealing with my nearly pathological resistance to guns, which I wouldn't mind avoiding a while longer, but—

"Now!" she says, marching towards the truck.

See what I mean, I think she's just too much for me.

CHAPTER TWO

YOU DON'T GO LOOKING for zombies, you just don't. Nobody does. You look for a place where the Zs aren't, where the Zs can't get to. Our little target practice was out on the Navajo reservation and I thought of taking us back to Cameron Trading Post, maybe ten miles away, but don't. I head us towards the Grand Canyon.

June notices. "Wasn't there a trading post just back there? We could try it."

I'm driving the beautiful, brand-new Toyota pickup I recently liberated, going slow down the road through the high desert, a long ridge of low lumpy hills to the left, the flat desert sloping down on our right with the Little Colorado River Gorge not far away. The land is a patchwork of brown and salmon and red, with low grass and sage brush.

"You didn't grow up in Arizona, did you?" I ask.

She shakes her head and I catch her frowning out of the corner of my eye. I've strayed into pre-apocalypse territory, but it's necessary this time.

"We're on the Navajo reservation," I say. "I just... Well, I kind of figure that somewhere out here they figured this zombie thing out.

They know how to grow corn in the desert and how to live in the heat with little water. They're probably doing better than the rest of the world. And... I..."

"You what?", she asks, her forehead crinkled in that cute way.

"Well, they have centuries of white men taking things from them." I shrug my shoulders, it's mostly a feeling and hard to express. "So... I don't want to go dissecting a Native American zombie."

She nods and is, I am sure, reappraising me. Probably thinking I'm filled with white man's guilt, even though everyone is equal now. The zombies don't discriminate, they want to munch on us all no matter the color of our skin, what our sexual preference is, or how much money we used to make.

June's skin has an olive tone, so maybe Italian heritage, or maybe Hispanic. With those blue eyes, though, it's hard to tell. Me, I'm decidedly white with sandy brown hair, a sprinkling of freckles, and a beard that's gotten longer than I like. Something I notice a lot more now that June is around.

"But haven't we been staying on the reservation?" she asks.

I shake my head. "Not strictly speaking. Wupatki is a national monument. We were on the rez when we went down to the river, but not for long."

She's studying me now. And yes, I'm not completely rational or clear about this. Wupatki worked because it was so empty; going to where the Navajo live out here doesn't feel right.

"So where to?" she asks.

"The Grand Canyon. The Desert View Overlook is not far and has a tower." I flash her a big grin and she groans. The last tower I took her to required that mad, manic bluff of the psychotic, petty, wannabe warlord. "There will have to be Zs there. Tourists. Lots of them."

She shakes her head and then checks her rifle.

CHAPTER THREE

DESERT VIEW IS my favorite overlook on the Grand Canyon. It was never the most popular one, those are all to the west around Grand Canyon Village. The canyon is not as deep at Desert View, despite it being the highest elevation overlook on the South Rim, but the view is spectacular.

It sits on Navajo Point where the Colorado River is making a sharp turn from the north to the west. You can see to the west into the deeper portion of the canyon and to the north into Marble Canyon, where it is not as deep but you can see the river for a long ways. You see the work of water on land, the slow erosion over millennia eroding away layer after layer, color after color, of rock. To the northeast, the desert is flat with mesas rising up, the land spotted with vegetation here and there, but mostly the tan to brown to red colors of the desert.

We cruise past the overlook turnoff a mile or so, we need to scout a bit before stopping, but we only see one Z in the distance at the crest of a hill off the road a bit. I turn us around, drive back, and pull into the Desert View turnoff and ease down toward the parking lot. The visibility isn't great here, the desert crowded with short, twisted juniper with shaggy silvery bark.

"My first time here," June says.

"You're gonna love it."

"We're here for a Z, remember? You're gonna show me this fungus brain thing, right?"

I nod. God, she's focused. The road in is clear and we make it to the big parking lot and I pull in at the far end where no cars are. Good visibility is what you always want.

I get out, feeling the weight of the gun holstered on my hip. I don't like it. I make sure the knife is on the other side, put my pack on, grab my baseball bat (I found a replacement during my all-night, save June prep session in Flagstaff), and snug down my Diamondback baseball cap. June gets her rifle and her pack. We never assume we are coming back. You just never know.

Things are spread out here. There's a small visitor's center and some bathrooms near the parking lot. Farther in there is a store and a snack bar, and right on the rim is the watchtower with an attached gift shop.

The air is warm and still as we move through the lot. The cars are a tangled mess at the other end with doors open, a pileup where one car rammed into another, and trash on the ground. I don't like it. I look to our right and there is another road and a gas station that I had forgotten about.

I signal to June and head that way. The time for chatting is when you are safe, not when you are hunting Zs.

The gas station is built in an adobe style with sand-brown walls and faux wood beams peeking out right below the flat roof. There are, surprisingly, no vehicles here. The glass door and windows of the convenience market are broken, and behind it is a tall, square garage and there are four pumps out front. We'll be needing to see if we can get any gas later.

We circle slowly, listening, and I think it's clear, we only see a few squirrels and the ever-present ravens. Just as we are about to head back to the front of the building, I hear banging coming from the garage. It's two bays with both garage doors closed. The doors have two sections of clear plastic starting about six feet up and going to the top of the door. I signal for June to wait and she readies her rifle. I slowly walk up and hear the snarl of a zombie. It increases in volume and the banging gets louder as I approach.

The Zs can sense the living. I'm not sure how, I'm really not. We are as quiet as can be and it can't smell us through that door, still it knows we are here. Whatever this sense is, I don't think their range is good, maybe a few hundred feet, but it is unnerving.

The Z slaps its leathery hand on the clear section of the door as I get close, and despite knowing it's there, I jump, my heart pounding in my head, adrenaline dumping into my bloodstream. I hold still, listening carefully until I am convinced it's only one Z, but boy is this one ripe.

I walk back to June.

"Only one," I whisper, "and probably there since the beginning. There could be things worth scavenging inside."

She nods and smiles.

"We need to go in the front, though. I don't think we can open that door from the outside."

We circle around and enter the cleaned-out convenience store, junk everywhere. We should pick through it later, someone might have missed something, but it doesn't look like it. To the right of the counter, there is a single metal door to the back and the Z is banging on it, knowing we are here now. It is surely starving over a year into the apocalypse and will be good to illustrate my fungus/parasite theory.

"Are you sure you want to do this?" I whisper.

Her blue eyes are hard as she nods.

And by "do this" I mean "risk our lives to kill a zombie and then dissect it to see if its brain has turned into a ball of fungus because the guy you met four days ago has a theory which in all probability is fueled by too many comic books as a kid and too many zombie movies and TV shows as an adult." But I don't say all that. She's stayed alive long enough to infer all but my self-doubts and recriminations. But, hey, she's known me for four days, so she probably gets that about me too.

We clear the junk out from in front of the door—can't have any tripping hazards in case we have to run—and I find a candy bar and hand it to her. She smiles, pockets it, and continues to clear a path to the door. We don't talk about this, we just do it. It makes me like her even more, that we don't have to discuss the basics of survival in the post-apocalyptic era.

It's tight, the door is right next to a wall, but it should work. She grabs the door handle with her left hand and has her gun in her right. I stand on the other side of the door, bat ready.

The Z is there, banging on the door, a pitiful whine interjecting here and there between the snarling. It almost sounds like a sad puppy for a moment, but the stink quickly dispels that image. I wrinkle my nose at the rotting meat smell and pull my T-shirt up over my nose. This one's going to stink.

I nod and June jerks open the door, using it to shield herself. The Z lurches out and the stench overwhelms me. It smells of rotting, putrid meat overlaid with a sharp spike of mold. My eyes water and I swing my bat down onto its head, hard. It's going to make a mess, but we need to crack open its skull anyway. It goes down in a heap. I drop my bat, kneel on its chest and knife it in the eye to make sure it's not coming back.

The Z is emaciated with dried-apple skin and is skeletally thin with wisps of black hair hanging on his head. He's dressed in filthy shorts and a T-shirt with what looks like a bite wound on his leathery arm. He must have been a tourist, gotten injured, and holed up here.

This Z and his poor condition reinforces my theory that Zs will "die" eventually if they don't have any food, but I can't think about it right now. I stand up, dizzy from the funk he's putting off, turn, rip my shirt off my nose, and puke on the floor.

June is too busy gagging and coughing to laugh at me. We both run out of the building gasping for breath.

"I hadn't counted on that... that..." she says before stumbling forward a few steps and puking.

I sit on the blacktop, pull out my water bottle and wash my mouth out and then offer it to June. I smile. It's actually a good day. I'm alive. I'm not alone. I have a purpose, of sorts, beyond survival. What's a little upset stomach and puke aftertaste balanced against actually being alive?

"What now?" she asks, sitting next to me.

I shrug my shoulders. "You want to look around while we wait for the stench to clear out? This is your first time here and it'd be a shame to miss it."

She looks back towards the store, her complexion just a tad green, and nods.

"Let's go look at that *tower*," I say nodding and smiling.

She shakes her head but smiles at me. No way we're going to get into trouble with every tower we encounter, is there?

CHAPTER FOUR

"OH, HELL," I mutter. From the gas station we took a service road, which quickly turned to gravel, ran along a side canyon, and we are behind the snack bar. It looks like there was a bloody last stand here some months ago.

We're in sight of the Desert View Watchtower, one of Mary Colter's masterpieces from the 1930s, a pueblo-style tower that gracefully tapers as it rises up seventy feet, made of irregular-sized, sandstone blocks with windows along the top. But the jumble of decomposing bodies is all we can look at.

It's been at least a few months and the bodies are dark, desiccated, and mummy-like where the flesh wasn't eaten by birds or bugs. White bones peek out from the gaps and holes in their sun-bleached tourist clothing. The smell isn't as a bad as the gas station Z, but it's a heavier, darker smell that creeps me out.

There's a group of ten or fifteen bodies piled up near two other bodies that are lying with their feet pointed towards each other six feet from the pile of Zs.

"Watch," June whispers, going closer.

She walks gently, her feet moving slow, coming down toe first as if she were a dancer. She takes guns off each of the two separated corpses, pulls some clips off them, and comes back to me.

She hands me one of the guns and three clips. "The pile is Zs. The other two offed each other instead of falling to them. A couple, I think."

It hits me, like a fist to the stomach. Intellectually I admire the act, although doubt I am capable of it. Emotionally... I just want to cry for them having to make that choice.

June has this distant look on her face and then she mumbles, "Now, that's love." I'm not even sure if she's talking to me. We don't say anything else but skirt the bodies and head towards the tower.

WE SKIRT the watchtower and the round, low gift shop connected to it and go to the lookout. We see more bodies, but nothing fresh and nothing moving. The gift shop is the same pueblo construction as the tower, about fifteen feet tall with larger windows.

The overlook is asphalt that has that never-cleaned look, covered with dirt and leaves, and is bordered by a metal railing. It's built on top of a huge hunk of Kaibab Limestone with Navajo Point below and the glory of the Canyon beyond.

And the view... the depth of the canyon to the west, the Colorado stretched out to the north, the canyon itself full of colors from light tan to deep umber in horizontal stripes that reveal the bones of the earth. This is the desert, so while there is vegetation, it's sparse, allowing the different geological layers of the canyon to be clearly seen. After the initial cliffs, the water has worn large structures out of the limestone and sandstone layers called mesas, buttes, and temples. And... well, if you've seen it you get it. If not, some are called temples because they look like these grand buildings or pyramids and the canyon seems like a holy place. The sun is headed towards the horizon, the yellow light deepening the already spectacular colors.

All the desiccated dead make it clear that the living aren't around, but we don't try the tower. We heard a bang on one of the large gift shop windows as we went by and saw a Z there staring at us. We looked at each other and just kept going. One Z, we can handle one Z. And any roamers would have been on us by now.

"Wow," June whispers when we reach the edge.

I take a deep breath and let it slowly out. "I know, right?" The Canyon has always given me such perspective. If you know how to read it, those rock layers show the history of the earth here going from millions to billions of years ago.

"Come on," I say, trotting back towards the path and scrambling down around the edge of the fence. Last time I was here was with the family and there was no fence hopping allowed. It's clear plenty have done it, a fading trail on the sharp ridge leads down to a ship's prow-like protrusion that juts into the canyon.

Some adrenaline is still in our systems and that, I think, leads to me making that bad decision and June shrugging and following.

In my mind, this feels like a first date, almost like there hasn't been an apocalypse and I'm just showing a girl I like something special. Taking her off the beaten trail so she can get the full experience. Showing off a bit.

Whatever it is that drives us forth, we don't notice the impending doom until it's too late.

The watchtower gift shop is full of Zs—probably another group that took refuge in there. We're far enough away and there's enough wind that we don't hear them banging on the glass until they break it and the group spills out.

"Shit!" June shouts.

I look back and there are twenty or so escaping the gift shop, but there are forty more lurching past the tower towards us. Where the hell did they come from?

The Zs are at the railing, tumbling over it, a few going over the side, but most getting up and shambling toward us. The gift shop Zs are all leathery, like the gas station Z, and must be absolutely starving. It makes them quicker than your average zombie and even more determined. The other group isn't in great shape, but a little fresher; they must have been roaming and we just missed them.

In the old world, one stupid decision and you'd wake up with a hangover, or get a traffic ticket, or maybe blow your rent money. Now? One dumb mistake and you die.

There is no escape here. The sides aren't sheer, but they are steep and sweep down hundreds of feet. We don't think about it. We run.

CHAPTER FIVE

WE'RE at the end of the trail on a rock jutting out with sheer drops on all sides. I stare as the horde descends, shuffling over the tan, sandy path, winding in and out of the yellowish limestone rocks and scraggly juniper trees. When the path narrows, a few lose their footing and fall into the canyon, but plenty are getting through.

They are hungry, their groans and snarls almost plaintive, their jaws snapping and teeth cracking, the sound of it getting louder as they approach.

"You gonna use that gun now?" she asks, her breath coming fast and a small smile on her sweating face.

Flashes of my childhood living room and my father's gun flicker past. The cold weight of the gun. The ear-piercing sound of it going off. The screams of my baby brother and the blood pouring down his arm.

I nod, the past is the past. I stuff my bat between my pack and my back and pull the 9mm. "These last few days have been—" I begin, but she cuts me off with a sharp shake of her head.

"Later," she whispers, a flicker of fear passing over her blue eyes, her mouth open and lips parted. The moment lasts less than a second and then the fear is gone and she's turned towards the Zs and is firing.

You know what? She's not just cute, she's beautiful, and if we're going to die a horrible death, shouldn't I at least try to kiss her?

No! Absolutely not. Are you crazy? What kind of guy do you think I am? It has occurred to me by this point that not only do I not know if she *likes* me, I don't know if she likes men. An attempt at a kiss would not only be colossally stupid, it might afford me a quick death where she kicks me in the balls and shoves me off the cliff, my last living thoughts being what a dumbass I am before the rocks below break my body.

I don't do that. I turn. I fire.

"Try to drop them all in one spot to block the path," she shouts as she drops her rifle and pulls a pistol. My ears are ringing and I can barely hear her.

I nod and think about that couple we just found, the ones that made sure they wouldn't be zombies. Yeah, I know I was just thinking of kissing her and now I'm wondering whether we should both just end it. But there's no time. I keep firing until the clip runs out, reload and fire again. I'm doing my best, but often miss the zombies, much less their heads. June is doing good and the bodies are starting to pile up, but it's not going to be enough. Not nearly enough.

CHAPTER SIX

THEY'RE BREAKING THROUGH. Most of the dead ones fall off the trail and go tumbling down into the canyon when they're shot. The "block the path" plan is not working. There are too many. They are almost on us.

Things don't slow down in a clichéd-movie-slow-mo-mode like at the dog food plant, but my brain seems to speed up. I suck with a gun. I'm great with a bat. I drop my gun, pull the bat and step forward, right in front of June.

She stops firing, thank God, and I am just on our side of the narrowest portion of the path. They can only come at us one at a time. So I swing and I swing and I swing. I don't have to connect with their heads, I just have to knock them off.

I've got my feet planted wide as I swing, lowering my center of gravity. It's a bit awkward, not like when you're up to bat, because I need to swing both ways, even though the backswing feels weird and weak. June comes up behind me, gets down low, and shoots at them between my legs.

Bam! A blow to the shoulder knocks a chubby tourist Z over the edge, its tattered flip-flops the last thing I see. June takes the next one down with a head shot, a small splatter of zombie yuck hitting me in the face.

Whack! A hit to the head of a former soccer mom and zombie goo goes everywhere. "Home run!" I say with as much humor as I can muster amidst the stink, the carnage, and the goo.

The next one shambles forward, too quick for my backswing, but June takes its knee out and it stumbles and I connect solidly with its midsection and it slowly slides over, its leathery hands grabbing my boot. I ignore it, the next one is on me.

Bam! A sloppy blow to the shoulder is enough to knock a little girl Z down, but she gets back up, and as much as I hate it, I swing hard for her head and knock her over the cliff. Meanwhile, June shoots the one clinging to my boot point-blank, the top of its head flying off, soon followed by the body, bouncing down the cliff.

The moment takes me, my breath loud in my head, sweat trickling down my back and slicking my hands. It's just the bat and the Zs. Flickers of stories try to invade my head, but I push them out. The Japanese man with the expensive DSLR camera around his neck, seeing the canyon for the first time. The tired Midwest mom getting one last family vacation in before the kids start going to college. The boy Z with earphones still in his ears that would have rather played video games than walk along one of the greatest wonders of this planet. The little girl frightened of heights, but bravely going to the rim only to be trapped there when the infection took hold here.

They used to be alive with lives and stories, hopes and fears, and bills and jobs. I push their stories away, the ones I imagine. They aren't alive, they are the dead. I swing and swing and swing, inelegant grunts escaping me.

The sun is hot and my nose is full of their rotting flesh, moldy funkiness, my face and arms and clothes covered in their splatter. My ears are full of their snarling sound and snapping jaws, the sharp crack of gunfire, the sound of breath being dragged into my tight chest. My breath is coming in gasps and sweat is dripping into my eyes. Jesus, how many tourists were up here when this thing started?

The bat is like a lead weight in my hand and I'm getting dizzy, my hands so sweaty I can barely hold it. There are more, but I can't do it. Is it time to ask June to put one of those bullets in my head? Is it time to grab her hand and the two of us just jump off?

I don't want to die, but I really, truly don't want to become a Z.

But I keep swinging even though I'm getting clumsy, pushing them off more by luck than skill, off balance and lurching a bit, looking something like a zombie myself. I start babbling more, mumbling "Home run," when I hit one good or "Foul ball," when I screw up. If you saw it, you might think this was more boy trying to impress girl on a first date, but really I'm just trying to keep myself focused, keep the bat swinging.

"Ground ball," I say between gritted teeth after a weak, grazing hit that has me off balance. I stumble, the long steep slope so many Zs have gone down ready to swallow me, my breath catching, and I know this is it. But June grabs me by the pack, jerks me back, and I go down in a heap. She steps forward, pistols in both hands firing one after the other. Bang. Bang. Bang.

She is simply magnificent, Linda Hamilton's Sarah Connor ain't got a thing on her.

She does it.

The last one goes down and she collapses next to me.

"Good... good job," I gasp out.

"You too, Slugger."

"Baseball... I used to play a lot of baseball."

She smiles weakly. "It shows."

I wait, thinking she might give me something, some little tidbit about her past, kind of like "I was a spy for Israel, I'm with the Mossad." But nothing, we sit there under the sun as we recover.

But those blue eyes and olive skin. I mean, she could be Israeli. And with that shooting, she could be Mossad.

CHAPTER SEVEN

WE MAKE it to the top of a tower. Finally.

Just as the sun is getting ready to set and the view can't get any better, we settle in on the top of Desert View Watchtower. We picked off a few more stragglers along the way, but nothing too difficult.

The inside of the tower is as much a masterpiece as the outside, but we rush up the stairs that twist around the tower wall. We gawk at the beautiful Hopi murals and reproduction of petroglyphs, our hands clinging to the leather wrapped handrail. We marvel at the circular openings between some levels that create an air of spaciousness and the rounded adobe-style treatment of all surfaces. Up we go through a final sloped ladder on the top level, through a trapdoor, and out onto a glorious zombie-free roof high above the ground below.

Despite the beauty of the inside, we rush, longing for the safety of the top of the tower, to be truly safe from the Zs. We rush for the view of the sun setting. We rush for the promise of a moment of peace and real sleep.

What I think happened is our scouting west of the overlook where we saw the one wandering Z caught the attention of that little

horde, we got their zombie senses tingling, and they roused themselves and came after us. At the same time, walking past the gift shop
got that group's attention. I'm thinking that the zombie fresh-flesh
detector thing is more like a hundred yards. I also think these old
zombies took some time to rouse themselves and didn't start banging
until we were too far away to hear.

"Here you go, Slugger," she says, handing me half of the candy
bar I found in the gas station. We've completed a quick meal of dog
food—any calories in an apocalypse—and a little chocolate is just
what I need. We had a meal like this when we met. Maybe it's
becoming our thing, Woody and June chasing dog food with chocolate on top of a roof.

"Thanks, Connor," I say.

"Sarah Connor?" she asks. "Like from the *Terminator*?"

I smile, delighted that she got the reference. "Yeah, you were
amazing."

She looks down, shakes her head, smiles, takes a bite of chocolate,
and looks back at the sunset settling over the Grand Canyon.

There are things to do, like see what kind of supplies we can find
around here, and see if my fungus-head zombie theory is correct. And
we've things to talk about, like whether June likes me, or boys for that
matter, but I leave most of it for later. We've got a place to sleep,
really sleep, the Zs can't get up here. We can relax, at least for a few
hours.

"Can I explain something?" I ask after dessert is over.

She nods but frowns.

It takes me a while to get it out, but I tell her about my little
brother and the shooting accident.

"Did he..." she says, a look of horror on her face.

"Oh... no," I say, feeling bad for leaving that part out. "Joshua
survived. The bullet barely missed an artery and nicked his bone and
his arm was never great after that. No baseball for him, but he
survived."

She nods and takes my hand and squeezes it. "It was just an accident. You were only a kid."

I nod, but the guilt still lies on me heavy.

I can see that she wants to ask me about Josh, if I know where he is, but she doesn't and I don't volunteer. I am still reluctant to go too deep into the past if it's not needed. Too much has been lost and sometimes the only way to deal with a deep loss is to ignore it—well, for as long as you can.

"But, you know, it's time to get good with a gun," she says sweetly. "Right?"

"Yeah, I guess it is."

I watch her for a bit as she watches the sun set. She's too much for me, that's for sure, and not just because of the guns. She's a complicated and strong woman that is still a mystery to me. And that's okay.

"You see there," I say, pointing to the north, "that deep gorge that is entering the canyon."

She nods and I'm not looking at her, but I see it out of the corner of my eye. I take a deep breath of her scent, sweaty and sweet.

"That's the Little Colorado River Gorge," I say. "Where it enters the Grand. We saw another piece of it where you were teaching me to shoot."

She nods again, her eyes drinking in the beauty of the tableau.

"The gorge is around three thousand feet deep there. The area is sacred to the Hopi. They believe that their ancestors emerged from a place near there called the *Sipapuni*."

In some ways I'm hoping this helps her understand my reluctance to mess with Native American zombies. I'm also trying to impress my decidedly cute companion. But, mostly, I'm just trying to help her enjoy what she's seeing.

It's more than just rock and water and the effects of time. It's vast and majestic, the land so beautiful it's not surprising there are those that consider it sacred.

I happen to be one of those people.

We're silent for a while and she grabs my hand and holds it, and the setting sun deepens the rich colors.

We sit there holding hands in one of the most beautiful places on earth watching the play of light and shadow. Who knows what tomorrow will bring, but for tonight I've got beauty in front of me, beauty sitting beside me, food in my belly, and a safe place to sleep.

Even before the Zs came, it really didn't get any better than this.

I watch June as she watches the sun set, eager to see what tomorrow will bring and what new facet she will reveal.

EPISODE 3

WOODY AND JUNE VERSUS THE GRAND CANYON

More adventure, more zombies, and more Woody and June awaits you in.... *Woody and June versus the Grand Canyon*.

Coming soon on May 8, 2019

Join the Woody and June Fan Club at WoodyAndJune.com so you don't miss a thing (plus fun behind-the-scenes features and free stuff!).

WOODY AND JUNE VERSUS THE GRAND CANYON

If the Z's Don't Get You, the Canyon Will

When Woody Beckman meets June Medina, neither expects the adventures that will follow. Dedicated go-it-alone survivors, they've learned not to trust anyone in post-zombie-apocalypse Arizona.

When the tourist zombie horde finds Woody and June, they have no choice but to run and only one place to go, but can they survive the Grand Canyon while being chased by an unstoppable undead force?

Will they outrun the zombies and survive the Grand Canyon long enough to find out what's next with their relationship?

A story of adventure and love and taking things (even the apocalypse) in stride.

ABOUT THE AUTHOR

Robert J. McCarter is the author of six novels, three novellas, and dozens of short stories. He is a finalist for the *Writers of the Future* contest and his stories have appeared in *The Saturday Evening Post, Adomeda Spaceways Inflight Magazine, Everyday Fiction*, and numerous anthologies.

He has written a series of first person ghost novels (starting with Shuffled Off: A Ghost's Memoir) and a superhero / love story series (Neutrinoman and Lightningirl, A Love Story), as well as two short story collections.

Of his latest novel, *Seeing Forever*, Kirkus Reviews says, "Sci-fi as it should be: engaging, moving, and grand in scope."

Find out more at:
robertjmccarter.com

BOOKS BY ROBERT J. MCCARTER

WOODY AND JUNE VERSUS THE APOCALYPSE

1. Woody and June versus the Wannabe Warlord
2. Woody and June versus the Fungus-Head Zombies
3. Woody and June versus the Grand Canyon (*coming May, 2019*)
4. Woody and June versus the Ex (*coming June, 2019*)
5. Woody and June versus the Third Wheel (*coming July, 2019*)
6. Woody and June versus Phantom Company (*coming August, 2019*)
7. Woody and June versus the Daring Rescue (*coming September, 2019*)

Join the Woody and June Fan Club at WoodyAndJune.com

NOVELS IN THE "GHOST'S MEMOIR" WORLD:

- Shuffled Off: A Ghost's Memoir, Book 1
- Drawing the Dead
- To Be a Fool: A Ghost's Memoir, Book 2
- Of Things Not Seen: A Ghost's Memoir, Book 3

OTHER NOVELS:

- Seeing Forever

BOOKS IN THE NEUTRINOMAN AND LIGHTNINGIRL SERIES:

- Meteor Attack! Neutrinoman and Lightningirl, A Love Story. Episode 1
- Toxic Asset: Neutrinoman and Lightningirl, A Love Story. Episode 2
- Protocol X: Neutrinoman and Lightningirl, A Love Story. Episode 3
- Season 1 (Omnibus edition of Episodes 1 - 3)
- Off Book: Neutrinoman and Lightningirl, A Love Story. Episode 4 (*Coming soon*)

WALTER ANCHOR, GHOST DETECTIVE STORIES

- **Case 1: "Detecting Haley"** (part of *Life After: Stories of Life, Death, and the Places in Between*)
- **Case 2: "The Ghost Brides Gift"** (exclusive to newsletter subscribers)
- **Case 3: "A Long Hard Fall"** (coming in 2019)

For a complete list of Walter Anchor stories, go to RobertJMcCarter.com/WalterAnchor

SHORT STORES AND COLLECTIONS

- Life After: Stories of Life, Death, and the Places in

Between

- Anomalous Readings: Thirteen Curious and Confounding Tales
- Probability: Resolve
- The Turing Test Will Be Televised
- Ghost Hacker, Zombie Maker

For a complete list, go to RobertJMcCarter.com